BOOTH TARKINGTON

MONSIEUR
BEAUCAIRE

DOUBLEDAY & COMPANY, INC.

Garden City, New York

PRINTED IN THE UNITED STATES OF AMERICA

To
H. T. J.
B. T.

The Decorations of this Book
were designed by
Chas. Edw. Hooper.

INTRODUCTION

Where are the romances of yester year? Dead as a door nail, most of them. Though indeed some of them do continue to survive, in an obscure existence like former beaux fallen upon shady days, in the cheap reprint editions of past favourites. And a very few, like *Hugh Wynne*, yet wear the dignity of enduring character. But, in general, now to run over a list of the titles of these one time pampered pets of the reading world brings such a smile as it does to recall song hits of other days: "Only a Bird in a Gilded Cage," "My Sweetheart's the Man in the Moon,"

INTRODUCTION

and "Down Went McGinty to the Bottom of the Sea." And it is indeed interesting to remark that the briefest, lightest, and slightest in effect of all that dashing throng has been among the very, very few to retain something like its virgin flush of rose. *Monsieur Beaucaire* the world has not so willingly let die. It continues to be kept "in stock" at book stores, and sells (I am told) if not in quantities, at least right along to-day; and it is continually being "drawn" from the shelves of public libraries. There is no difficulty about the explanation: no work of perfect art is ever permitted to perish altogether. And, though perhaps a bit flamboyant in manner, I do not know that it is a particularly hazardous observation to say to *Beaucaire:*

x

When old age shall this generation waste,
  Thou shalt remain, in midst of other woe
Than ours, a friend to man, to whom thou
    say'st,
  "Beauty is truth, truth beauty,—that is all
  Ye know on earth, and all ye need to
  know."

At any rate, let us not be niggardly of appreciation in the presence of a tiny bit of well-nigh flawless beauty. *Monsieur Beaucaire* ought to last (let us say) as long as there is a taste for *The Master of Ballantrae.*

Monsieur Beaucaire has been compared to the art of Watteau. And this comparison, an inevitable one and a kind of inspiration, is the happiest of the many that have been made. It is a comparison which is constructive criticism. M. Camille Mauclair in his little study, both lyric and penetrating,

of Watteau, speaks of those celebrated
fêtes galantes as "tender, dazzling, and
most deliciously aristocratic." Exactly
so, *Beaucaire*, that vivid, pastel-like
sketch of a flashing episode in the life
of a "small, fair gentleman," radiant,
exquisite of heart, brilliant, audacious,
winningly dignified, a French duke of
the royal blood at Bath in the eigh-
teenth century; who masquerades, for
his private purposes, in this resort of
white-satin-sheen fashion first as a
"gamblist" barber, and then as the
Duc de Chateaurien, laughing in his
sleeve at the dull-witted Englishman
who, incited by the Duke of Winterset's personal animosity, tries to hunt
him down as a *laquais;* who falls under
the spell of "gold and snow and the
blue sky of a lady's eye," the Beauty of

Bath,—"*bellissima*, divine, *glorieuse !*"
and who shows by his sword that he is
one "born." A tale, or something less
than a tale, whose only, and complete,
excuse for its being is the blitheness of
its mood, the symmetry of its form, the
iridescent colour of its words, the swift-
ness of its action, and the tingling vital-
ity of it, from start to finish; a thing of
dainty wit all compact.

One of the perpetual delights of
Monsieur Beaucaire is the crispness
with which its sparkling and rapidly
shifting scenes are realized. The reader
actually sees as clearly as though he had
before him a painting by the late
Howard Pyle, or a drawing by Daniel
Vierge, the picture given of the chairmen swarming in the street at Lady
Malbourne's door, "where the joyous

vulgar fought with muddled footmen
and tipsy link-boys for places of vantage whence to catch a glimpse of
quality and of raiment at its utmost.
Dawn was in the east, and the guests
were departing." Or, again, view that
night of the "stately junket," when
"all of Bath that pretended to fashion
or condition was present at a *fête* at the
house of a country gentleman of the
neighborhood:"

There fell a clear September night,
when the moon was radiant over town
and country, over cobbled streets and
winding roads. From the fields the
mists rose slowly, and the air was mild
and fragrant, while distances were
white and full of mystery.

Then it was that the coach took the

road with the happy Frenchman riding
close to that adorable window which
framed the fairest face in England, a
dozen gallants riding before, when a
wild halloo sounded ahead; the horn
wound loudly, and, with drawn swords
flashing in the moon, a party of horsemen charged down the highway, their
cries blasting the night,—and the battle
was joined. Or see Beau Nash standing "at the door of the rooms, smiling
blandly upon a dainty throng in the
pink of its finery and gay furbelows."
Best of all, the scene in the Pump Room
where Monsieur Beaucaire's identity is
disclosed by the arrival of his brother
and the French Ambassador, to the
consternation of his enemies and still
more of the Lady Mary Carlisle, who
had loved him until she was taught to

scorn him as a servant,—a scene in which are mingled bright charm and subtle pathos.

He offered his hand to Lady Mary. "Mademoiselle is fatigué. Will she honour me?"

He walked with her to the door, her hand fluttering faintly in his. From somewhere about the garments of one of them a little cloud of faded rose-leaves fell, and lay strewn on the floor behind them. He opened the door, and the lights shone on a multitude of eager faces turned toward it. There was a great hum of voices, and, over all, the fiddles wove a wandering air, a sweet French song of the *voyageur*.

He bowed very low, as, with fixed and glistening eyes, Lady Mary Carlisle, the Beauty of Bath, passed slowly by him and went out of the room.

Ye gods! as Mr. Baxter says, *that* is the air of Romance.

ROBERT CORTES HOLLIDAY.

Chapter
One

THE young Frenchman did very well what he had planned to do. His guess that the Duke would cheat proved good. As the unshod half-dozen figures that had been standing noiselessly in the entryway stole softly into the shadows of the chamber, he leaned across the table and smilingly plucked a card out of the big Englishman's sleeve.

"Merci, M. le Duc!" he laughed, rising and stepping back from the table.

The Englishman cried out, "It means the dirty work of silencing you with my bare hands!" and came at him.

"Do not move," said M. Beaucaire, so sharply that the other paused. "Observe behind you."

The Englishman turned, and saw what trap he had blundered into; then stood transfixed, impotent, alternately scarlet with rage and white with the vital shame of discovery. M. Beaucaire remarked, indicating the silent figures by a polite wave of the hand, "Is it not a compliment to monsieur that I procure six large men to subdue him? They are quite de-

2

vote' to me, and monsieur is alone.
Could it be that he did not wish even
his lackeys to know he play with the
yo'ng Frenchman who Meestaire
Nash does not like in the pomp-
room? Monsieur is unfortunate to
have come on foot and alone to my
apartment."

The Duke's mouth foamed over
with chaotic revilement. His captor
smiled brightly, and made a slight
gesture, as one who brushes aside a
boisterous insect. With the same
motion he quelled to stony quiet a
resentful impetus of his servants toward the Englishman.

"It's murder, is it, you carrion!"
finished the Duke.

M. Beaucaire lifted his shoulders
in a mock shiver. "What words!

3

No, no, no! No killing! A such
word to a such host! No, no, not
mur-r-der; only disgrace!" He
laughed a clear, light laugh with a
rising inflection, seeming to launch
himself upon an adventurous quest for
sympathy.

"You little devilish scullion!" spat
out the Duke.

"Tut, tut! But I forget. Monsieur has pursue' his studies of deportment amongs' his fellow-country-
men."

"Do you dream a soul in Bath
will take your word that I—that
I——"

"That M. le Duc de Winterset had
a card up his sleeve?"

"You pitiful stroller, you stable-
boy, born in a stable——"

4

"Is it not an honor to be born where monsieur must have been bred?"

"You scurvy foot-boy, you greasy barber, you cutthroat groom——"

"Overwhelm'!" The young man bowed with imperturbable elation. "M. le Duc appoint' me to all the office' of his househol'."

"You mustachioed fool, there are not five people of quality in Bath will speak to you——"

"No, monsieur, not on the parade; but how many come to play with me here? Because I will play always, night or day, for what one will, for any long, and al—ways fair, monsieur."

"You outrageous varlet! Every one knows you came to England as the French Ambassador's barber.

5

What man of fashion will listen to you? Who will believe you?"

"All people, monsieur. Do you think I have not calculate', that I shall make a failure of my little en. terprise?"

"Bah!"

"Will monsieur not reseat him-self?" M. Beaucaire made a low bow. "So. We must not be too tire' for Lady Malbourne's rout. Ha, ha! And you, Jean, Victor, and you others, retire; go in the hallway. Attend at the entrance, François. So; now we shall talk. Monsieur, I wish you to think very cool. Then listen; I will be briefly. It is that I am well known to be all, entire' hones'. Gamblist? Ah, yes; true and mos' profitable; but fair, al—ways fair;

6

every one say that. Is it not so?
Think of it. And—is there never a
w'isper come to M. le Duc that not
all people belief him to play al—ways
hones'? Ha, ha! Did it almos' be
said to him las' year, after when he
play' with Milor' Tappin'ford at the
chocolate-house——"

"You dirty scandal-monger!" the
Duke burst out. "J'll——"

"Monsieur, monsieur!" said the
Frenchman. "It is a poor valor to
insult a helpless captor. Can he re-
tort upon his own victim? But it is
for you to think of what I say.
True, I am not reco'nize on the parade; that my frien's who come here
do not present me to their ladies;
that Meestaire Nash has reboff' me
in the pomp-room; still, am I not

7

known for being hones' and fair in
my play, and will I *not* be belief',
even I, when I lif' my voice and
charge you aloud with what is already w'isper'? Think of it! You
are a noble, and there will be some
hang-dogs who might not fall away
from you. Only such would be lef'
to you. Do you want it tol'? And
you can keep out of France, monsieur? I have lef' his service, but I
have still the ear of M. de Mirepoix,
and he know' I never lie. Not a
gentleman will play you when you
come to Paris."

The Englishman's white lip showed
a row of scarlet dots upon it. "How
much do you want?" he said.

The room rang with the gay
laughter of Beaucaire. "I hol' your

note' for seven-hunder' pound'. You
can have them, monsieur. Why does
a such great man come to play M.
Beaucaire? Because no one else will-
in' to play M. le Duc—he cannot
pay. Ha, ha! So he come' to good
Monsieur Beaucaire. Money, ha,
ha! What I want with money?"

His Grace of Winterset's features
were set awry to a sinister pattern.
He sat glaring at his companion in a
snarling silence.

"Money? Pouf!" snapped the
little gambler. "No, no, no! It is
that M. le Duc, impoverish', somewhat in a bad odor as he is, yet com-
mand the *entrée any*-where—onless
I— Ha, ha! Eh, monsieur?"

"Ha! You dare think to force
me——"

M. Beaucaire twirled the tip of his slender mustache around the end of his white forefinger. Then he said: "Monsieur and me goin' to Lady Malbourne's ball to-night—M. le Duc and me!"

The Englishman roared, "Curse your impudence!"

"Sit quiet. Oh, yes, that's all; we goin' together."

"No!"

"Certain. I make all my little plan'. 'Tis all arrange'." He paused, and then said gravely, "You goin' present me to Lady Mary Carlisle."

The other laughed in utter scorn. "Lady Mary Carlisle, of all women alive, would be the first to prefer the devil to a man of no birth, barber."

"'Tis all arrange'; have no fear;

nobody question monsieur'
You goin' take me to-night—
"No!"

"Yes. And after—then *I* have the *entrée*. Is it much I ask? This one little favor, and I never w'isper, never breathe that—it is to say, I am always forever silent of monsieur's misfortune."

"*You* have the *entrée!*" sneered the other. "Go to a lackeys' rout and dance with the kitchen maids. If I would, I could not present you to Bath society. I should have cartels from the fathers, brothers, and lovers of every wench and madam in the place, even I. You would be thrust from Lady Malbourne's door five minutes after you entered it."

"No, no, no!"

"Half the gentlemen in Bath have been here to play. They would know you, wouldn't they, fool? You've had thousands out of Bantison, Rakell, Guilford, and Townbrake. They would have you lashed by the grooms as your ugly deserts are. *You* to speak to Lady Mary Carlisle! 'Od's blood! You! Also, dolt, she would know you if you escaped the others. She stood within a yard of you when Nash expelled you the pump-room."

M. Beaucaire flushed slightly. "You think I did not see?" he asked.

"Do you dream that because Winterset introduces a low fellow he will be tolerated—that Bath will receive a barber?"

12

"I have the distinction to call monsieur's attention," replied the young man gayly, "I have renounce' that profession."

"Fool!"

"I am now a man of honor!"

"Faugh!"

"A man of the parts," continued the the young Frenchman, "and of deportment; is it not so? Have you seen me of a fluster, or gross ever, or, what sall I say—*bourgeois?* Shall you be shame' for your guest' manner? No, no! And my appearance, is it of the people? Clearly, no. Do I not compare in taste of apparel with your yo'ng Englishman? Ha, ha! To be hope'. Ha, ha! So I am goin' talk with Lady Mary Carlisle."

"Bah!" The Duke made a savage burlesque. "'Lady Mary Carlisle, may I assume the honor of presenting the barber of the Marquis de Mirepoix?' So, is it?"

"No, monsieur," smiled the young man. "Quite not so. You shall have nothing to worry you, nothing in the worl'. I am goin' to assassinate my poor mustachio—also remove this horrible black peruke, and emerge in my own hair. Behol'!" He swept the heavy curled, mass from his head as he spoke, and his hair, coiled under the great wig, fell to his shoulders, and sparkled yellow in the candle-light. He tossed his head to shake the hair back from his cheeks. "When it is dress', I am transform'; nobody can know me; you shall ob-

14

serve. See how little I ask of you,
how very little bit. No one shall rec-
o'nize 'M. Beaucaire' or 'Victor.'
Ha, ha! 'Tis all arrange'; you have
nothing to fear."

"Curse you," said the Duke, "do
you think I'm going to be saddled
with you wherever I go as long as
you choose?"

"A mistake. No. All I requi—
All I beg—is this one evening. 'Tis
all shall be necessary. *After*, I shall
not need monsieur."

"Take heed to yourself—after!"
vouchsafed the Englishman between
his teeth.

"Conquered!" cried M. Beau-
caire, and clapped his hands gleefully.
"Conquered for the night! Aha, it
is riz'nable! I shall meet what you

15.

send—after. One cannot hope too much of your patience. It is but natural you should attemp' a little avengement for the rascal trap I was such a wicked fellow as to set for you. I shall meet some strange frien's of yours after to-night; not so? I must try to be not too much frighten'." He looked at the Duke curiously. "You want to know why I create this tragedy, why I am so unkind as to entrap monsieur?"

His Grace of Winterset replied with a chill glance; a pulse in the nobleman's cheek beat less relentlessly; his eye raged not so bitterly; the steady purple of his own color was returning; his voice was less hoarse; he was regaining his habit. "'Tis ever the manner of the vulgar," he observed, "to wish to be seen with people of fashion."

"Oh, no, no, no!" The Frenchman laughed. " 'Tis not that. Am I not already one of these 'men of fashion'? I lack only the reputation of birth. Monsieur is goin' supply that. Ha, ha! I shall be noble from to-night. 'Victor,' the artis', is condemn' to death; his throat shall be cut with his own razor. 'M. Beaucaire'—" Here the young man sprang to his feet, caught up the black wig, clapped into it a dice-box from the table, and hurled it violently through the open door. "'M. Beaucaire' shall be choke' with his own dice-box. Who is the Phœnix to remain? What advantage have I not over other men of rank who are

17

merely born to it? I may choose my own. No! Choose for me, monsieur. Shall I be chevalier, comte, vicomte, marquis, what? None. Out of compliment to monsieur can I wish to be anything he is not? No, no! I shall be M. le Duc, M. le Duc de—de Chateaurien. Ha, ha! You see? You are my *confrère*."

M. Beaucaire trod a dainty step or two, waving his hand politely to the Duke, as though in invitation to join the celebration of his rank. The Englishman watched, his eye still and harsh, already gathering in craftiness. Beaucaire stopped suddenly. "But how I forget my age! I am twenty-three," he said, with a sigh. "I rejoice too much to be of the quality. It has been too great for me, and I

had always belief' myself free of such
ambition. I thought it was enough
to behol' the opera without wishing
to sing; but no, England have teach'
me I have those vulgar desire'. Monsieur, I am goin' tell you a secret:
the ladies of your country are very
diff'runt than ours. One may adore
the demoiselle, one must worship the
lady of England. Our ladies have the
—it is the beauty of youth; yours remain comely at thirty. Ours are
flowers, yours are stars! See, I betray myself, I am so poor a patriot.
And there is one among these stars—
ah, yes, there is one—the poor Frenchman has observe' from his humble
distance; even there he could bask in
the glowing!" M. Beaucaire turned
to the window, and looked out into

the dark. He did not see the lights
of the town. When he turned again,
he had half forgotten his prisoner;
other pictures were before him.

"Ah, what radiance!" he cried.
"Those people up over the sky, they
want to show they wish the earth to
be happy, so they smile, and make
this lady. Gold-haired, an angel of
heaven, and yet a Diana of the chase!
I see her fly by me on her great
horse one day; she touch' his mane
with her fingers. I buy that clipping
from the groom. I have it here with
my dear brother's picture. Ah, *you!*
Oh, yes, you laugh! What do you
know! 'Twas all I could get. But
I have heard of the endeavor of M.
le Duc to recoup his fortunes. This
alliance shall fail. It is not the way

—that heritage shall be safe' from him! It is you and me, monsieur! You can laugh! The war is open', and by *me!* There is one great step taken: until to-night there was nothing for you to ruin, to-morrow you have got a noble of France—your own *protégé*—to besiege and sack. And you are to lose, because you think such ruin easy, and because you understand nothing—far less—of divinity. How could you know? You have not the fiber; the heart of a lady is a blank to you; you know nothing of the vibration. There are some words that were made only to tell of Lady Mary, for her alone— *bellissima,* divine, *glorieuse!* Ah, how I have watch' her! It is sad to me when I see her surround' by your

yo'ng captains, your nobles, your rat-
tles, your beaux—ha, ha!—and I
mus' hol' far aloof. It is sad for me
—but oh, jus' to watch her and to
wonder! Strange it is, but I have almos' cry out with rapture at a look I
have see' her give another man, so
beautiful it was, so tender, so dazzling
of the eyes and so mirthful of the
lips. Ah, divine coquetry! A look
for another, *ah-i-me!* for many others; and even to you, one day, a rose,
while I—I, monsieur, could not even
be so blessed as to be the groun' beneath her little shoe! But *to-night*,
monsieur—ha, ha!—*to-night*, monsieur, you and me, two princes, M. le
Duc de Winterset and M. le Duc de
Chateaurien—ha, ha! you see?—we
are goin' arm-in-arm to that ball, and

I am goin' have one of those looks, *I!* And a rose! *I!* It is time. But ten minute', monsieur. I make my apology to keep you waitin' so long while I go in the nex' room and execute my poor mustachio—that will be my only murder for jus' this one evening—and inves' myself in white satin. Ha, ha! I shall be very gran', monsieur. François, send Louis to me; Victor, to order two chairs for monsieur and me; we are goin' out in the worl' to-night!"

Chapter Two

HE chairmen swarmed in the street at Lady Malbourne's door, where the joyous vulgar fought with muddled footmen and tipsy link-boys for places of vantage whence to catch a glimpse of quality and of raiment at its utmost. Dawn was in the east, and the guests were departing. Singly or in pairs, glittering in finery, they came mincing down the steps, the ghost of the night's smirk fading to jadedness as they sought the dark recesses of their chairs. From within sounded the twang of fiddles still swinging manfully at it, and the windows were bright with the light of many candles. When the door was flung open to call the chair of Lady Mary Carlisle, there was an eager pressure of the throng to see.

A small, fair gentleman in white satin came out upon the steps, turned and bowed before a lady who appeared in the doorway, a lady whose royal loveliness was given to view for a moment in that glowing frame. The crowd sent up a hearty English cheer for the Beauty of Bath.

The gentleman smiled upon them delightedly. "What enchanting peo-

ple!" he cried. "Why did I not
know, so I might have shout' with
them?" The lady noticed the people not at all; whereat, being pleased,
the people cheered again. The gentleman offered her his hand; she
made a slow courtesy; placed the tips
of her fingers upon his own. "I
am honored, M. de Chateaurien," she
said.

"No, no!" he cried earnestly.
"Behol' a poor Frenchman whom
emperors should envy." Then rever-
ently and with the pride of his gal-
lant office vibrant in every line of his
light figure, invested in white satin
and very grand, as he had prophesied,
M. le Duc de Chateaurien handed
Lady Mary Carlisle down the steps,
an achievement which had figured in

the ambitions of seven other gentlemen during the evening.

"Am I to be lef' in such on-
happiness?" he said in a low voice.
"That rose I have beg' for so
long——"

"Never!" said Lady Mary.

"Ah, I do not deserve it. I know
so well! But——"

"Never!"

"It is the greatness of my on-
worthiness that alone can claim your
charity; let your kin' heart give this
little red rose, this great alms, to the
poor beggar."

"Never!"

She was seated in the chair. "Ah,
give the rose," he whispered. Her
beauty shone dazzlingly on him out of
the dimness.

"Never!" she flashed defiantly as she was closed in. "Never!"

"Ah!"

"Never!"

The rose fell at his feet.

"A rose lasts till morning," said a voice behind him.

Turning, M. de Chateaurien looked beamingly upon the face of the Duke of Winterset.

"'Tis already the daylight," he replied, pointing to the east. "Monsieur, was it not enough honor for you to han' out madame, the aunt of Lady Mary? Lady Rellerton retain' much trace of beauty. 'Tis strange you did not appear more happy."

"The rose is of an unlucky color, I think," observed the Duke.

"The color of a blush, my brother."

"Unlucky, I still maintain," said the other calmly.

"The color of the veins of a Frenchman. Ha, ha!" cried the young man. "What price would be too high? A rose is a rose! A good-night, my brother, a good-night. I wish you dreams of roses, red roses, only beautiful red, red roses!"

"Stay! Did you see the look she gave these street folk when they shouted for her? And how are you higher than they, when she knows? As high as yonder horse-boy!"

"Red roses, my brother, only roses. I wish you dreams of red, red roses!"

WAS well agreed by
the fashion of Bath
that M. le Duc de
Chateaurien was a per-
son of sensibility and
haut ton; that his retinue and equipage
surpassed in elegance; that his person
was exquisite, his manner engaging.
In the company of gentlemen his
ease was slightly tinged with gra-
ciousness (his single equal in Bath being his Grace of Winterset); but it

was remarked that when he bowed over a lady's hand, his air bespoke only a gay and tender reverence.

He was the idol of the dowagers within a week after his appearance; matrons warmed to him; young belles looked sweetly on him, while the gentlemen were won to admiration or envy. He was of prodigious wealth: old Mr. Bicksit, who dared not, for his fame's sake, fail to have seen all things, had visited Chateaurien under the present Duke's father, and descanted to the curious upon its grandeurs. The young noble had one fault, he was so poor a gambler. He cared nothing for the hazards of a die or the turn of a card. Gayly admitting that he had been born with no spirit of adventure in him, he was sure, he declared, that he failed of much happiness by his lack of taste in such matters.

But he was not long wanting the occasion to prove his taste in the matter of handling a weapon. A certain led-captain, Rohrer by name, notorious, amongst other things, for bearing a dexterous and bloodthirsty blade, came to Bath post-haste, one night, and jostled heartily against him in the pump-room on the following morning. M. de Chauteaurien bowed, and turned aside without offense, continuing a conversation with some gentlemen near by. Captain Rohrer jostled against him a second time. M. de Chateaurien looked him in the eye, and apologized pleasantly for being so much in the way. Thereupon

32

Rohrer procured an introduction to him, and made some observations derogatory to the valor and virtue of the French.

There was current a curious piece of gossip of the French court: a prince of the blood royal, grandson of the late Regent and second in the line of succession to the throne of France, had rebelled against the authority of Louis XV, who had commanded him to marry the Princess Henriette, cousin to both of them. The princess was reported to be openly devoted to the cousin who refused to accept her hand at the bidding of the king; and, as rumor ran, the prince's caprice elected in preference the discipline of Vincennes, to which retirement the furious king had consigned him. The story was the staple gossip of all polite Europe; and Captain Rohrer, having in his mind a purpose to make use of it in leading up to a statement that should be general to the damage of all Frenchwomen, and which a Frenchman might not pass over as he might a jog of the elbow, repeated it with garbled truths to make a scandal of a story which bore none on a plain rela-, tion.

He did not reach his deduction. M. de Chateaurien, breaking into his narrative, addressed him very quietly. "Monsieur," he said, "none but swine deny the nobleness of that good and gentle lady, Mademoiselle la Princesse de Bourbon-Conti. Every Frenchman know' that her cousin is

a bad rebel and ingrate, who had only
honor and rispec' for her, but was so
wilful he could not let even the king
say, 'You shall marry here, you shall
marry there.' My frien's," the young
man turned to the others, "may I ask
you to close roun' in a circle for one
moment? It is clearly shown that
the Duke of Orleans is a scurvy fellow, but not—" he wheeled about
and touched Captain Rohrer on the
brow with the back of his gloved
hand—"but not so scurvy as thou,
thou swine of the gutter!"

Two hours later, with perfect ease,
he ran Captain Rohrer through the
left shoulder—after which he sent a
basket of red roses to the Duke of
Winterset. In a few days he had
another captain to fight. This was a

35

ruffling buck who had the astounding
indiscretion to proclaim M. de Chateaurien an impostor. There was no
Chateaurien, he swore. The Frenchman laughed in his face, and, at twi-
light of the same day, pinked him
carefully through the right shoulder.
It was not that he could not put aside
the insult to himself, he declared to
Mr. Molyneux, his second, and the
few witnesses, as he handed his wet
sword to his lackey—one of his station could not be insulted by a doubt
of that station—but he fought in the
quarrel of his friend Winterset. This
rascal had asserted that M. le Duc
had introduced an impostor. Could
he overlook the insult to a friend, one
to whom he owed his kind recep-
tion in Bath? Then, bending over

36.

his fallen adversary, he whispered: "Naughty man, tell your master find some better quarrel for the nex' he sen' agains' me."

The conduct of M. de Chateaurien was pronounced admirable.

There was no surprise when the young foreigner fell naturally into the long train of followers of the beautiful Lady Mary Carlisle, nor was there great astonishment that he should obtain marked favor in her eyes, shown so plainly that my Lord Townbrake, Sir Hugh Guilford, and the rich Squire Bantison, all of whom had followed her through three seasons, swore with rage, and his Grace of Winterset stalked from her aunt's house with black brows.

Meeting the Duke there on the

evening after his second encounter
de Chateaurien smiled upon him brilliantly. "It was badly done; *oh*, so
badly!" he whispered.   "Can you
afford to have me strip' of my mask
by any but yourself? You, who introduce' me? They will say there is
some bad scandal that I could force
you to be my god-father. You mus'
get the courage yourself."

   'I told you a rose had a short
life," was the answer.

   "Oh, those roses! 'Tis the very
greates' rizzon to gather each day a
fresh one." He took a red bud from
his breast for an instant, and touched
it to his lips.

   "M. de Chateaurien!"   It was
Lady Mary's voice; she stood at a
table where a vacant place had been

left beside her. "M. de Chateaurien, we have been waiting very long for you."

The Duke saw the look she did not know she gave the Frenchman, and he lost countenance for a moment.

"We approach a climax, eh, monsieur?" said M. de Chateaurien.

Chapter
Four

THERE fell a clear September night, when the moon was radiant over town and country, over cobbled streets and winding roads. From the fields the mists rose slowly, and the air was mild and fragrant, while distances were white and full of mystery. All of Bath that pretended to fashion or condition was present that evening at a *fête* at the house of a

country gentleman of the neighborhood. When the stately junket was
concluded, it was the pleasure of M.
de Chateaurien to form one of the
escort of Lady Mary's carriage for the
return. As they took the road, Sir
Hugh Guilford and Mr. Bantison, en-.
gaging in indistinct but vigorous re-
monstrance with Mr. Molyneux over
some matter, fell fifty or more paces
behind, where they continued to ride,
keeping up their argument. Half a
dozen other gallants rode in advance,
muttering among themselves, or at-
tended laxly upon Lady Mary's aunt
on the other side of the coach, while
the happy Frenchman was permitted
to ride close to that adorable window
which framed the fairest face in England.

41

He sang for her a little French song, a song of the *voyageur* who dreamed of home. The lady, listening, looking up at the bright moon, felt a warm drop upon her cheek, and he saw the tears sparkling upon her lashes.

"Mademoiselle," he whispered then, "I, too, have been a wanderer, but my dreams were not of France; no, I do not dream of that home, of that dear country. It is of a dearer country, a dream country—a country of gold and snow," he cried softly, looking at her white brow and the fair, lightly powdered hair above it. "Gold and snow, and the blue sky of a lady's eyes!"

"I had thought the ladies of France were dark, sir."

"Cruel! It is that she will not understan'! Have I speak of the ladies of France? No, no, no! It is of the faires' country; yes, 'tis a province of heaven, mademoiselle. Do I not renounce my allegiance to France? Oh, yes! I am subjec'— no, content to be slave—in the lan' of the blue sky, the gold, and the snow."

"A very pretty figure," answered Lady Mary, her eyes downcast. "But does it not hint a notable experience in the making of such speeches?"

"Tormentress! No. It prove' only the inspiration it is to know you."

"We English ladies hear plenty of the like sir; and we even grow brilliant enough to detect the assurance

43

that lies beneath the courtesies of our
own gallants."

"*Merci!* I should believe so!"
ejaculated M. de Chateaurien; but he
smothered the words upon his lips.

Her eyes were not lifted. She
went on: "We come, in time, to believe that true feeling comes faltering
forth, not glibly; that smoothness
betokens the adept in the art, sir,
rather than your true—your true—"
She was herself faltering; more, blush-
ing deeply, and halting to a full stop
in terror of a word. There was a
silence.

"Your—true—lover," he said hus-
kily. When he had said that word
both trembled. She turned half away
into the darkness of the coach.

"I know what make' you to doubt

me," he said, faltering himself, though it was not his art that prompted him. "They have tol' you the French do nothing al—ways but make love, is it not so? Yes, you think *I* am like that. You think I am like that now!"

She made no sign.

"I suppose," he sighed, "I am un-riz'nable; I would have the snow not so col'—for jus' me."

She did not answer.

"Turn to me," he said.

The fragrance of the fields came to them, and from the distance the faint, clear note of a hunting-horn.

"Turn to me."

The lovely head was bent very low. Her little gloved hand lay upon the narrow window ledge. He laid his

45

own gently upon it. The two hands
were shaking like twin leaves in the
breeze. Hers was not drawn away.
After a pause, neither knew how
long, he felt the warm fingers turn
and clasp themselves tremulously
about his own. At last she looked
up bravely and met his eyes. The
horn was wound again—nearer.

"All the cold was gone from the
snows—long ago," she said.

"My beautiful!" he whispered;
it was all he could say. "My beautiful!" But she clutched his arm,
startled.

"*'Ware the road!*" A wild halloo
sounded ahead. The horn wound
loudly. "*'Ware the road!*" There
sprang up out of the night a flying
thunder of hoof-beats. The gentle-

46

men riding idly in front of the coach
scattered to the hedge-sides; and,
with drawn swords flashing in the
moon, a party of horsemen charged
down the highway, their cries blasting the night.

"Barber! Kill the barber!" they
screamed. "Barber! Kill the barber!"

Beaucaire had but time to draw
his sword when they were upon him.

"*A moi!*" his voice rang out clearly
as he rose in his stirrups. "*A moi*,
François, Louis, Berquin! *A moi*,
François!"

The cavaliers came straight at him.
He parried the thrust of the first, but
the shock of collision hurled his horse
against the side of the coach.

"Sacred swine!" he cried bitterly. "To endanger a lady, to make this brawl in a lady's presence! Drive on!" he shouted.

"No!" cried Lady Mary.

The Frenchman's assailants were masked, but they were not highwaymen. "Barber! Barber!" they shouted hoarsely, and closed in on him in a circle.

"See how he use his steel!" laughed M. Beaucaire, as his point passed through a tawdry waistcoat. For a moment he cut through the ring and cleared a space about him, and Lady Mary saw his face shining in the moonlight. "*Canaille!*" he hissed, as his horse sank beneath him; and, though guarding his head from the rain of blows from above, he managed to drag headlong from his sad dle the man who had hamstrung the poor brute. The fellow came suddenly to the ground, and lay there.

"Is it not a compliment," said a heavy voice, "to bring six large men to subdue monsieur?"

"Oh, you are there, my frien'! In the rear—a little in the rear, I think. Ha, ha!"

The Frenchman's play with his weapon was a revelation of skill, the nore extraordinary as he held in his hand only a light dress sword. But the ring closed about him, and his keen defense could not avail him for more than a few moments. Lady Mary's outriders, the gallants of her escort, rode up close to the coach and encircled it, not interfering.

40

"Sir Hugh Guilford!" cried Lady Mary wildly, "if you will not help him, give me your sword!" She would have leaped to the ground, but Sir Hugh held the door.

"Sit quiet, madam," he said to her; then, to the man on the box, "Drive on."

"If he does, I'll kill him!" she said fiercely. "Ah, what cowards! Will you see the Duke murdered?"

"The Duke!" laughed Guilford. "They will not kill him, unless—be easy, dear madam, 'twill be explained. Gad's life!" he muttered to Molyneux, "'Twere time the varlet had his lashing! D'ye hear her?"

"Barber or no barber," answered Molyneux, "I wish I had warned him. He fights as few gentlemen could. Ah—ah! Look at that! 'Tis a shame!"

On foot, his hat gone, his white coat sadly rent and gashed, flecked, too, with red, M. Beaucaire, wary, alert, brilliant, seemed to transform himself into a dozen fencing-masters; and, though his skill appeared to lie in delicacy and quickness, his play being continually with the point, sheer strength failed to beat him down. The young man was laughing like a child.

"Believe me," said Molyneux, "he's no barber! No, and never was!"

For a moment there was even a chance that M. Beaucaire might have the best of it. Two of his adversaries were prostrate, more than one were groaning, and the indomitable Frenchman had actually almost beat off the ruffians, when, by a trick, he was overcome. One of them, dismounting, ran in suddenly from behind, and seized his blade in a thick leather gauntlet. Before Beaucaire could disengage the weapon, two others threw themselves from their horses and hurled him to the earth. "*À moi! À moi*, François!" he cried as he went down, his sword in fragments, but his voice unbroken and clear.

"Shame!" muttered one or two of the gentlemen about the coach.

" 'Twas dastardly to take him so," said Molyneux. "Whatever his deservings, I'm nigh of a mind to offer him a rescue in the Duke's face."

"Truss him up, lads," said the

heavy voice. "Clear the way in front
of the coach. There sit those whom
we avenge upon a presumptuous
lackey. Now, Whiffen, you have a
fair audience, lay on and baste him."

Two men began to drag M. Beaucaire toward a great oak by the roadside. Another took from his saddle
a heavy whip with three thongs.

"*A moi, François!*"

There was borne on the breeze
an answer—"*Monseigneur! Monseigneur!*" The cry grew louder suddenly. The clatter of hoofs urged
to an anguish of speed sounded on the
night. M. Beaucaire's servants had
lagged sorely behind, but they made
up for it now. Almost before the
noise of their own steeds they came
riding down the moonlit aisle be-

tween the mists. Chosen men, these
servants of Beaucaire, and like a
thunderbolt they fell upon the astounded cavaliers.

"Chateaurien! Chateaurien!" they
shouted, and smote so swiftly that,
through lack of time, they showed
no proper judgment, discriminating
nothing between non-combatants and
their master's foes. They charged
first into the group about M. Beaucaire, and broke and routed it utterly.
Two of them leaped to the young
man's side, while the other four,
swerving, scarce losing the momen-
tum of their onset, bore on upon the
gentlemen near the coach, who went
down beneath the fierceness of the
onslaught, cursing manfully.

"Our just deserts," said Mr. Molyneux, his mouth full of dust and phi-losophy.

Sir Hugh Guilford's horse fell with him, being literally ridden over, and the baronet's leg was pinned under the saddle. In less than ten minutes from the first attack on M. Beaucaire, the attacking party had fled in disorder, and the patrician non-combatants, choking with expletives, consumed with wrath, were prisoners, disarmed by the Frenchman's lackeys.

Guilford's discomfiture had freed the doors of the coach; so it was that when M. Beaucaire, struggling to rise, assisted by his servants, threw out one hand to balance himself, he found it seized between two small, cold palms, and he looked into two warm, dilating eyes, that were doubly beautiful because of the fright and rage that found room in them, too.

M. le Duc Chateaurien sprang to his feet without the aid of his lackeys, and bowed low before Lady Mary.

"I make ten thousan' apology to be˘ the cause of a such *mêlée* in your presence," he said; and then, turning to François, he spoke in French: "Ah, thou scoundrel! A little, and it had been too late."

François knelt in the dust before him. "Pardon!" he said. "Monseigneur commanded us to follow far in the rear, to remain unobserved. The wind malignantly blew against monseigneur's voice."

"See what it might have cost, my children," said his master, pointing to the ropes with which they would have bound him and to the whip lying beside them. A shudder passed over the lackey's frame; the utter horror in his face echoed in the eyes of his fellows.

"Oh, monseigneur!" François sprang back, and tossed his arms to heaven.

"But it did not happen," said M. Beaucaire.

"It could not!" exclaimed François.

"No. And you did very well, my children—" the young man smiled benevolently—"very well. And now," he continued, turning to Lady Mary and speaking in English, "let me be asking of our gallants yonder what make' them to be in cabal with highwaymen. One should come to a

57

polite understanding with them, you think? Not so?"

He bowed, offering his hand to conduct her to the coach, where Molyneux and his companions, having drawn Sir Hugh from under his horse, were engaged in reviving and reassuring Lady Rellerton, who had fainted. But Lady Mary stayed Beaucaire with a gesture, and the two stood where they were.

"Monseigneur!" she said, with a note of raillery in her voice, but raillery so tender that he started with happiness. His movement brought him a hot spasm of pain, and he clapped his hand to a red stain on his waistcoat.

"You are hurt!"

"It is nothing," smiled M. Beau-

caire. Then, that she might not see
the stain spreading, he held his handkerchief over the spot. "I am a
little—but jus' a trifling—bruise';
'tis all."

"You shall ride in the coach," she
whispered. "Will you be pleased,
M. de Chateaurien?"

"Ah, my beautiful!" She seemed
to wave before him like a shining
mist. "I wish that ride might las'
for al—ways! Can you say that,
mademoiselle?"

"Monseigneur," she cried in a pas-
sion of admiration, "I would what
you would have be, should be. What
do you not deserve? You are the
bravest man in the world!"

"Ha, ha! I am jus' a poor Frenchman."

"Would that a few Englishmen had shown themselves as 'poor' to-night. The vile cowards, not to help you!" With that, suddenly possessed by her anger, she swept away from him to the coach.

Sir Hugh, groaning loudly, was being assisted into the vehicle.

"My little poltroons," she said, "what are you doing with your fellow-craven, Sir Hugh Guilford, there?"

"Madam," replied Molyneux humbly, "Sir Hugh's leg is broken. Lady Rellerton graciously permits him to be taken in."

"*I* do not permit it! M. de Chateaurien rides with us."

"But——"

"Sir! Leave the wretch to groan

by the roadside," she cried fiercely,
"which plight I would were that of
all of you! But there will be a pretty
story for the gossips to-morrow! And
I could almost find pity for you when
I think of the wits when you return
to town. Fine gentlemen you; hardy'
bravos, by heaven! to leave one man
to meet a troop of horse single-
handed, while you huddle in shelter
until you are overthrown and disarmed by servants! Oh, the wits!
Heaven save you from the wits!"

"Madam."

"Address me no more! M. de
Chateaurien, Lady Rellerton and I
will greatly esteem the honor of your
company. Will you come?"

She stepped quickly into the coach,
and was gathering her skirts to make

room for the Frenchman, when a
heavy voice spoke from the shadows
of the tree by the wayside.

"Lady Mary Carlisle will, no
doubt, listen to a word of counsel on
this point."

The Duke of Winterset rode out
into the moonlight, composedly un-
tieing a mask from about his head.
He had not shared the flight of his
followers, but had retired into the
shade of the oak, whence he now
made his presence known with the
utmost coolness.

"Gracious heavens, 'tis Winterset!" exclaimed Lady Rellerton.

"Turned highwayman and cut-
throat," cried Lady Mary.

"No, no," laughed M. Beaucaire,
somewhat unsteadily, as he stood,

swaying a little, with one hand on the coach-door, the other pressed hard on his side, "he only oversee'; he is jus' a little bashful, sometime'. He is a great man, but he don' want *all* the glory!"

"Barber," replied the Duke, "I must tell you that I gladly descend to bandy words with you; your monstrous impudence is a claim to rank I cannot ignore. But a lackey who has himself followed by six other lackeys——"

"Ha, ha! Has not M. le Duc been busy all this evening to justify me? And I think mine mus' be the bes' six. Ha, ha! You think?"

"M. de Chateaurien," said Lady Mary, "we are waiting for you."

"Pardon," he replied. "He has

something to say; maybe it is bes' if
you hear it now."

"I wish to hear nothing from him
—ever!"

"My faith, madam," cried the
Duke, "this saucy fellow has paid
you the last insult! He is so sure of
you he does not fear you will believe
the truth. When all is told, if you
do not agree he deserved the lashing
we planned to——"

"I'll hear no more!"

"You will bitterly repent it,
madam. For your own sake I en-
treat——"

"And I also," broke in M. Beaucaire. "Permit me, mademoiselle;
let him speak."

"Then let him be brief," said
Lady Mary, "for I am earnest to

be quit of him. His explanation of
an attack on my friend and on my
carriage should be made to my
brother."

"Alas that he was not here," said
the Duke, "to aid me! Madam,
was your carriage threatened? I have
endeavored only to expunge a debt I
owed to Bath and to avenge an insult
offered to yourself through——"

"Sir, sir, my patience will bear
little more!"

"A thousan' apology," said M.
Beaucaire. "You will listen, I only
beg, Lady Mary?"

She made an angry gesture of
assent.

"Madam, I will be brief as I may.
Two months ago there came to Bath
a French gambler calling himself

Beaucaire, a desperate fellow with the cards or dice, and all the men of fashion went to play at his lodging, where he won considerable sums. He was small, wore a black wig and mustachio. He had the insolence to show himself everywhere until the Master of Ceremonies rebuffed him in the pump-room, as you know, and after that he forbore his visits to the rooms. Mr. Nash explained (and was confirmed, madam, by indubitable information) that this Beaucaire was a man of unspeakable, vile, low birth, being, in fact, no other than a lackey of the French king's ambassador, Victor by name, de Mirepoix's barber. Although his condition was known, the hideous impudence of the fellow did not desert him, and he remained in Bath, where none would speak to him."

"Is your farrago nigh done, sir?"

"A few moments, madam. One evening, three weeks gone, I observed a very elegant equipage draw up to my door, and the Duke of Chateaurien was announced. The young man's manners were worthy— according to the French acceptance —and 'twere idle to deny him the most monstrous assurance. He declared himself a noble traveling for pleasure. He had taken lodgings in Bath for a season, he said, and called at once to pay his respects to me. His tone was so candid—in truth, I am the simplest of men, very easily gulled—and his stroke so bold, that I did not for one moment suspect him;

67

and, to my poignant regret—though in the humblest spirit I have shown myself eager to atone—that very evening I had the shame of presenting him to yourself."

"The shame, sir!"

"Have patience, pray, madam. Ay, the shame! You know what figure he hath cut in Bath since that evening. All ran merrily with him until several days ago Captain Badger denounced him as an impostor, vowing that Chateaurien was nothing."

"Pardon," interrupted M. Beaucaire. "'Castle Nowhere' would have been so much better. Why did you not make him say it that way, monsieur?"

Lady Mary started; she was looking at the Duke, and her face was white. He continued: "Poor Captain Badger was stabbed that same day——"

"Most befitting poor Captain Badger," muttered Molyneux.

"——And his adversary had the marvelous insolence to declare that he fought in *my* quarrel! This afternoon the wounded man sent for me, and imparted a very horrifying intelligence. He had discovered a lackey whom he had seen waiting upon Beaucaire in attendance at the door of this Chateaurien's lodging. Beaucaire had disappeared the day before Chateaurien's arrival. Captain Badger looked closely at Chateaurien at their next meeting, and identified him with the missing Beaucaire beyond the faintest doubt. Overcome

69

with indignation, he immediately
proclaimed the impostor. Out of
regard for me, he did not charge him
with being Beaucaire; the poor soul
was unwilling to put upon me the
humiliation of having introduced a
barber; but the secret weighed upon
him till he sent for me and put
everything in my hands. I accepted
the odium; thinking only of atone-
ment. I went to Sir John Wimpledon's *fête*. I took poor Sir Hugh,
there, and these other gentlemen
aside, and told them my news. We
narrowly observed this man, and were
shocked at our simplicity in not having discovered him before. These
are men of honor and cool judgment,
madam. Mr. Molyneux had acted
for him in the affair of Captain

Badger, and was strongly prejudiced in his favor; but Mr. Molyneux, Sir Hugh, Mr. Bantison, every one of them, in short, recognized him. In spite of his smooth face and his light hair, the adventurer Beaucaire was writ upon him amazing plain. Look at him, madam, if he will dare the inspection. You saw this Beaucaire well, the day of his expulsion from the rooms. Is not this he?"

M. Beaucaire stepped close to her. Her pale face twitched.

"Look!" he said.

"Oh, oh!" she whispered with a dry throat, and fell back in the carriage.

"Is it so?" cried the Duke.

"I do not know.—I—cannot tell."

"One moment more. I begged

these gentlemen to allow me to wipe
out the insult I had unhappily offered
to Bath, but particularly to you.
They agreed not to forestall me or to
interfere. I left Sir John Wimpledon's
early, and arranged to give the sorry
rascal a lashing under your own eyes,
a satisfaction due the lady into whose
presence he had dared to force himself."

"'*Noblesse oblige*'?" said M. Beaucaire in a tone of gentle inquiry.

"And now, madam," said the
Duke, "I will detain you not one
second longer. I plead the good
purpose of my intentions, begging
you to believe that the desire to
avenge a hateful outrage, next to the
wish to serve you, forms the dearest
motive in the heart of Winterset."

"Bravo!" cried Beaucaire softly.

Lady Mary leaned toward him, a thriving terror in her eyes. "It is false?" she faltered.

"Monsieur should not have been born so high. He could have made little book'."

"You mean it is false?" she cried breathlessly.

"'Od's blood, is she not convinced?" broke out Mr. Bantison. "Fellow, were you not the ambassador's barber?"

"It is all false?" she whispered.

"The mos' fine art, mademoiselle. How long you think it take M. de Winterset to learn that speech after he write it out? It is a mix of what is true and the mos' chaste art. Monsieur has become a man of letters.

73

Perhaps he may enjoy that more than the wars. Ha, ha!"

Mr. Bantison burst into a roar of laughter. "Do French gentlemen fight lackeys? Ho, ho, ho! A pretty country! We English do as was done to-night, have our servants beat them."

"And attend ourselves," added M. Beaucaire, looking at the Duke, "somewhat in the background? But, pardon," he mocked, "that remind' me. François, return to Mr. Bantison and these gentlemen their weapons."

"Will you answer a question?" said Molyneux mildly.

"Oh, with pleasure, monsieur."

"Were you ever a barber?"

"No, monsieur," laughed the young man.

74

"Pah!" exclaimed Bantison. "Let me question him. Now, fellow, a confession may save you from jail. Do you deny you are Beaucaire?"

"Deny to a such judge?"

"Ha!" said Bantison. "What more do you want, Molyneux? Fellow, do you deny that you came to London in the ambassador's suite?"

"No, I do not deny."

"He admits it! Didn't you come as his barber?"

"Yes, my frien', as his barber."

Lady Mary cried out faintly, and, shuddering, put both hands over her eyes.

"I'm sorry," said Molyneux. "You fight like a gentleman."

"I thank you, monsieur."

75

"You called yourself Beaucaire?"

"Yes, monsieur." He was swaying to and fro; his servants ran to support him.

"I wish—" continued Molyneux, hesitating. "Evil take me!—but I'm sorry you're hurt."

"Assist Sir Hugh into my carriage," said Lady Mary.

"Farewell, mademoiselle!" M. Beaucaire's voice was very faint. His eyes were fixed upon her face. She did not look toward him.

They were propping Sir Hugh on the cushions. The Duke rode up close to Beaucaire, but François seized his bridle fiercely, and forced the horse back on its haunches.

"The man's servants worship him," said Molyneux.

76

"Curse your insolence!" exclaimed the Duke. "How much am I to bear from this varlet and his varlets? Beaucaire, if you have not left Bath by to-morrow noon, you will be clapped into jail, and the lashing you escaped to-night shall be given you thrice tenfold!"

"I shall be—in the—Assembly—Room' at nine—o'clock, one week —-from—to-night," answered the young man, smiling jauntily, though his lips were colorless. The words cost him nearly all his breath and strength. "You mus' keep—in the —-backgroun', monsieur. Ha, ha!"

The door of the coach closed with slam.

"Mademoiselle—fare—well!"

"Drive on!" said Lady Mary.

M. Beaucaire followed the carriage with his eyes. As the noise of the wheels and the hoof-beats of the accompanying cavalcade grew fainter in the distance, the handkerchief he had held against his side dropped into the white dust, a heavy red splotch.

"Only—roses," he gasped, and fell back in the arms of his servants.

Chapter
Five

BEAU NASH stood at the door of the rooms, smiling blandly upon a dainty throng in the pink of its finery and gay furbelows. The great exquisite bent his body constantly in a series of consummately adjusted bows: before a great dowager, seeming to sweep the floor in august deference; somewhat stately to the young bucks; greeting the wits with gracious friendliness and a twinkle of raillery; inclining with fatherly gallantry before the beauties; the degree of his inclination measured the altitude of the recipient as accurately as a nicely calculated sand-glass measures the hours.

The King of Bath was happy, for wit, beauty, fashion—to speak more concretely: nobles, belles, gamesters, beaux, statesmen, and poets—made fairyland (or opera bouffe, at least) in his dominions; play ran higher and higher, and Mr. Nash's coffers filled up with gold. To crown his pleasure, a prince of the French blood, the young Comte de Beaujolais, just arrived from Paris, had reached Bath at noon in state, accompanied by the Marquis de Mire-

poix, the ambassador of Louis XV
The Beau dearly prized the society of
the lofty, and the present visit was an
honor to Bath: hence to the Master
of Ceremonies. What was better,
there would be some profitable hours
with the cards and dice. So it was
'that Mr. Nash smiled never more be-
nignly than on that bright evening.
The rooms rang with the silvery
voices of women and delightful
laughter, while the fiddles went merrily, their melodies chiming sweetly
with the joyance of his mood.

The skill and brazen effrontery of
the ambassador's scoundrelly servant
in passing himself off for a man of
condition formed the point of de-
parture for every conversation. It
was discovered that there were but

three persons present who had not
suspected him from the first; and, by
a singular paradox, the most astute of
all proved to be old Mr. Bicksit, the
traveler, once a visitor at Chateaurien; for he, according to report, had
by a coup of diplomacy entrapped the
impostor into an admission that there
was no such place. However, like
poor Captain Badger, the worthy old
man had held his peace out of regard
for the Duke of Winterset. This
nobleman, heretofore secretly dis-
liked, suspected of irregular devices
at play, and never admired, had won
admiration and popularity by his re-
morse for the mistake, and by the
modesty of his attitude in endeavor-
ing to atone for it, without presum-
ing upon the privilege of his rank to

laugh at the indignation of society;
an action the more praiseworthy
because his exposure of the impostor
entailed the disclosure of his own
culpability in having stood the villain's sponsor. To-night, the happy
gentleman, with Lady Mary Carlisle
upon his arm, went grandly about
the rooms, sowing and reaping a
harvest of smiles. 'Twas said work
would be begun at once to rebuild
the Duke's country seat, while several ruined Jews might be paid out
of prison. People gazing on the
beauty and the stately but modest
hero by her side, said they would
make a noble pair. She had long
been distinguished by his attentions,
and he had come brilliantly out of
the episode of the Frenchman, who

had been his only real rival. Wherever they went, there arose a buzz of pleasing gossip and adulation.

Mr. Nash, seeing them near him, came forward with greetings. A word on the side passed between the nobleman and the exquisite.

"'I had news of the rascal tonight," whispered Nash. "He lay at a farm till yesterday, when he disappeared; his ruffians, too."

"You have arranged?" asked the Duke.

"Fourteen bailiffs are watching without. He could not come within gunshot. If they clap eyes on him, they will hustle him to jail, and his cutthroats shall not avail him a hair's weight. The impertinent swore he'd be here by nine, did he?"

"He said so; and 'tis a rash dog, sir."

"It is just nine now."

"Send out to see if they have taken him."

"Gladly." The Beau beckoned an attendant, and whispered in his ear.

Many of the crowd had edged up to the two gentlemen with apparent carelessness, to overhear their conversation. Those who did overhear repeated it in covert asides, and this circulating undertone, confirming a vague rumor that Beaucaire would attempt the entrance that night, lent a pleasurable color of excitement to the evening. The French prince, the ambassador, and their suites were announced. Polite as the assembly was, it was also curious, and there occurred a mannerly rush to see the newcomers. Lady Mary, already pale, grew whiter as the throng closed round her; she looked up pathetically at the Duke, who lost no time in extricating her from the pressure.

"Wait here," he said; "I will fetch you a glass of negus," and disappeared. He had not thought to bring a chair, and she, looking about with an increasing faintness and finding none, saw that she was standing by the door of a small side-room. The crowd swerved back for the passage of the legate of France, and pressed upon her. She opened the door, and went in.

The room was empty save for two

gentlemen, who were quietly playing cards at a table. They looked up as she entered. They were M. Beaucaire and Mr. Molyneux.

She uttered a quick cry and leaned against the wall, her hand to her breast. Beaucaire, though white and weak, had brought her a chair before Molyneux could stir.

"Mademoiselle——"

"Do not touch me!" she said, with such frozen abhorrence in her voice that he stopped short. "Mr. Molyneux, you seek strange company!"

"Madam," replied Molyneux, bowing deeply, as much to Beaucaire as to herself, "I am honored by the presence of both of you."

"Oh, are you mad!" she exclaimed, contemptuously.

"This gentleman has exalted me with his confidence, madam," he replied.

"Will you add your ruin to the scandal of this fellow's presence here? How he obtained entrance—— "

"Pardon, mademoiselle," interrupted Beaucaire. "Did I not say I should come? M. Molyneux was so obliging as to answer for me to the fourteen frien's of M. de Winterset and *Meestaire* Nash."

"Do you not know," she turned vehemently upon Molyneux, "that he will be removed the moment I leave this room? Do you wish to be dragged out with him? For your sake, sir, because I have always thought you a man of heart, I give you a chance to save yourself from

88

disgrace—and—your companion from
jail. Let him slip out by some retired way, and you may give me
your arm and we will enter the next
room as if nothing had happened.
Come, sir——"

"Mademoiselle——"

"Mr. Molyneux, I desire to hear
nothing from your companion. Had
I not seen you at cards with him I
should have supposed him in attendance as your lackey. Do you desire
to take advantage of my offer, sir?"

"Mademoiselle, I could not tell
you, on that night——"

"You may inform your high-born
friend, Mr. Molyneux, that I heard
everything he had to say; that my
pride once had the pleasure of listening to his high-born confession!"

"Ah, it is gentle to taunt one with his birth, mademoiselle? Ah, no! There is a man in my country who say strange things of that—that a man is not his father, but *himself*."

"You may inform your friend, Mr. Molyneux, that he had a chance to defend himself against accusation; that he said all——"

"That I did say all I could have strength to say. Mademoiselle, you did not see—as it was right—that I had been stung by a big wasp. It was nothing, a scratch; but, mademoiselle, the sky went round and the moon dance' on the earth. I could not wish that big wasp to see he had stung me; so I mus' only say what I can have strength for, and stan' straight till he is gone. Beside',

there are other rizzons. Ah, you
mus' belief! My Molyneux I sen'
for, and tell him all, because he show
courtesy to the yo'ng Frenchman,
and I can trus' him. I trus' you,
mademoiselle—long ago—and would
have tol' you ev'rything, excep' jus'
because—well, for the romance, the
fon! You belief? It is so clearly
so; you do belief, mademoiselle?"

She did not even look at him. M.
Beaucaire lifted his hand appealingly
toward her. "Can there be no faith
in—in—" he said timidly, and
paused. She was silent, a statue, my
Lady Disdain.

"If you had not belief' me to be
an impostor; if I had never said I
was Chateaurien; if I had been jus'
that Monsieur Beaucaire of the story

they tol' you, but never with the
heart of a lackey, an hones' man, a
man, the man you knew, *himself*,
could you—would you—" He was
trying to speak firmly; yet, as he
gazed upon her splendid beauty, he
choked slightly, and fumbled in the
lace at his throat with unsteady fingers.—"Would you—have let me ride
by your side in the autumn moonlight?" Her glance passed by him as
it might have passed by a footman or
a piece of furniture. He was dressed
magnificently, a multitude of orders
glittering on his breast. Her eye
took no knowledge of him.

"Mademoiselle—I have the honor
to ask you: if you had known this
Beaucaire was hones', though of
peasant birth, would you——"

Involuntarily, controlled as her icy presence was, she shuddered. There was a moment of silence.

"Mr. Molyneux," said Lady Mary, "in spite of your discourtesy in allowing a servant to address me, I offer you a last chance to leave this room undisgraced. Will you give me your arm?"

"Pardon me, madam," said Mr. Molyneux.

Beaucaire dropped into a chair with his head bent low and his arm outstretched on the table; his eyes filled slowly in spite of himself, and two tears rolled down the young man's cheeks.

"An' live men are jus'—*names!*" said M. Beaucaire.

Chapter
Six

*I*N the outer room,
Winterset, unable to
find Lady Mary, and
supposing her to have
joined Lady Reller-
ton, disposed of his negus, then ap-
proached the two visitors to pay his
respects to the young prince, whom
he discovered to be a stripling of
seventeen, arrogant-looking, but pretty
as a girl. Standing beside the Marquis de Mirepoix—a man of quiet

bearing—he was surrounded by a group of the great, among whom Mr. Nash naturally counted himself. The Beau was felicitating himself that the foreigners had not arrived a week earlier, in which case he and Bath would have been detected in a piece of gross ignorance concerning the French nobility—making much of de Mirepoix's ex-barber.

"'Tis a lucky thing that fellow was got out of the way," he ejaculated, under cover.

"Thank me for it," rejoined Winterset.

An attendant begged Mr. Nash's notice. The head bailiff sent word that Beaucaire had long since entered the building by a side door. It was supposed Mr. Nash had known of it,

and the Frenchman was not arrested,
as Mr. Molyneux was in his company, and said he would be answerable
for him. Consternation was so plain
on the Beau's trained face that the
Duke leaned toward him anxiously.

"The villain's in, and Molyneux
hath gone mad!"

Mr. Bantison, who had been
fiercely elbowing his way toward
them, joined heads with them. "You
may well say he is in," he exclaimed,
"and if you want to know where,
why, in yonder card-room. I saw
him through the half-open door."

"What's to be done?" asked the
Beau.

"Send the bailiffs——"

"Fie, fie! A file of bailiffs? The
scandal!"

"Then listen to me," said the Duke. "I'll select half-a-dozen gentlemen, explain the matter, and we'll put him in the center of us and take him out to the bailiffs. 'Twill appear nothing. Do you remain here and keep the attention of Beaujolais and de Mirepoix. Come, Bantison, fetch Townbrake and Harry Rakell yonder; I'll bring the others."

Three minutes later, his Grace of Winterset flung wide the card-room door, and, after his friends had entered, closed it.

"Ah!" remarked M. Beaucaire quietly. "Six more large men."

The Duke, seeing Lady Mary, started; but the angry signs of her interview had not left her face, and reassured him. He offered his hand

97

to conduct her to the door. "May I have the honor?"

"If this is to be known, 'twill be better if I leave after; I should be observed if I went now."

"As you will, madam," he answered, not displeased. "And now, you impudent villain," he began, turning to M. Beaucaire, but to fall back astounded. "'Od's blood, the dog hath murdered and robbed some royal prince!" He forgot Lady Mary's presence in his excitement. "Lay hands on him!" he shouted. "Tear those orders from him!"

Molyneux threw himself between. "One word!" he cried. "One word before you offer an outrage you will repent all your lives!"

"Or let M. de Winterset come alone," laughed M. Beaucaire.

"Do you expect me to fight a cut-throat barber, and with bare hands?"

"I think one does not expec' monsieur to fight anybody. Would *I* fight you, you think? That was why I had my servants, that evening we play. I would gladly fight almos' any one in the worl'; but I did not wish to soil my hand with a——"

"Stuff his lying mouth with his orders!" shouted the Duke.

But Molyneux still held the gentlemen back. "One moment," he cried.

"M. de Winterset," said Beaucaire, "of what are you afraid? You calculate well. Beaucaire might have been belief'—an impostor that you yourself expose'? Never! But I was not goin' reveal that secret. You have not absolve me of my promise."

"Tell what you like," answered the Duke. "Tell all the wild lies you have time for. You have five minutes to make up your mind to go quietly."

"Now you absolve me, then? Ha, ha! Oh, yes! Mademoiselle," he bowed to Lady Mary, "I have the honor to reques' you leave the room. You shall miss no details if these frien's of yours kill me, on the honor of a French gentleman."

"A French what?" laughed Ban, tison.

"Do you dare keep up the pretense?" cried Lord Townbrake. "Know, you villain barber, that your

114

master, the Marquis de Mirepoix, is
in the next room."

Molyneux heaved a great sigh of
relief. "Shall I—" He turned to
M. Beaucaire.

The young man laughed, and said:
"Tell him come here at once."

"Impudent to the last!" cried
Bantison, as Molyneux hurried from
the room.

"Now you goin' to see M. Beaucaire's master," said Beaucaire to Lady
Mary. "'Tis true what I say, the other
night. I cross from France in his
suite; my passport say as his barber.
Then to pass the *ennui* of exile, I
come to Bath and play for what one
will. It kill the time. But when the
people hear I have been a servant
they come only secretly; and there is

one of them—he has absolve' me of
a promise not to speak—of him I
learn something he cannot wish to be
tol'. I make some trouble to learn
this thing. Why I should do this?
Well—that is my own rizzon. So I
make this man help me in a masque,
the unmasking it was, for, as there is
no one to know me, I throw off my
black wig and become myself—and
so I am 'Chateaurien,' Castle Nowhere. Then this man I use', this
Winterset, he——"

"I have great need to deny these
accusations?" said the Duke.

"Nay," said Lady Mary wearily.

"Shall I tell you why I mus' be
'Victor' and 'Beaucaire' and 'Chateaurien,' and not myself?"

"To escape from the bailiffs for

debts for razors and soap," gibed Lord Townbrake.

"No, monsieur. In France I have got a cousin who is a man with a very bad temper at some time', and he will never enjoy his relatives to do what he does not wish——"

He was interrupted by a loud commotion from without. The door was flung open, and the young Count of Beaujolais bounded in and threw his arms about the neck of M. Beaucaire.

"Philippe!" he cried. "My brother, I have come to take you back with me."

M. de Mirepoix followed him, bowing as a courtier, in deference; but M. Beaucaire took both his hands heartily. Molyneux came after, with Mr. Nash, and closed the door.

"My warmest felicitations," said the Marquis. "There is no longer need for your incognito."

"Thou best of masters!" said Beaucaire, touching him fondly on the shoulder. "I know. Your courier came safely. And so I am forgiven! But I forget." He turned to the lady. She had begun to tremble exceedingly. "Faires' of all the English fair," he said, as the gentlemen bowed low to her deep courtesy, "I beg the honor to presen' to Lady Mary Carlisle, M. le Comte de Beaujolais. M. de Mirepoix has already the honor. Lady Mary has been very kind to me, my frien's; you mus' help me make my acknowledgment. Mademoiselle and gentlemen, will you give

me that favour to detain you one
instan'?"

"Henri," he turned to the young
Beaujolais, "I wish you had shared
my masque—I have been so gay!"
The surface of his tone was merry,
but there was an undercurrent, weary-
sad, to speak of what was the mood,
not the manner. He made the effect
of addressing every one present, but
he looked steadily at Lady Mary.
Her eyes were fixed upon him,
with a silent and frightened fas-
cination, and she trembled more and
more. "I am a great actor, Henri.
These gentlemen are yet scarce con-
vince' I am not a lackey! And I mus'
tell you that I was jus' now to be expelled for having been a barber!"

"Oh, no!" the ambassador cried

out. "He would not be content with me; he would wander over a strange country."

"Ha, ha, my Mirepoix! And what is better, one evening I am oblige' to fight some frien's of M. de Winterset there, and some ladies and cavaliers look on, and they still think me a servant. Oh, I am a great actor! 'Tis true there is not a peasant in France who would not have then known one 'born'; but they are wonderful, this English people, holding by an idea once it is in their heads—a mos' worthy quality. But my good Molyneux here, he had speak to me with courtesy, jus' because I am a man an' jus' because he is al—ways kind. (I have learn' that his great-grandfather was a Frenchman.) So I sen' to him and tell him ev'rything, and he gain admittance for me here to-night to await my frien's.

"I was speaking to messieurs about my cousin, who will meddle in the affair' of his relative'. Well, that gentleman, he make a marriage for me with a good and accomplish' lady, very noble and very beautiful— and amiable." (The young count at his elbow started slightly at this, but immediately appeared to wrap himself in a mantle of solemn thought.) "Unfortunately, when my cousin arrange' so, I was a dolt, a little blockhead; I swear to marry for myself and when I please, or never if I like. That lady is all things charming and gentle, and, in truth, she is— very much attach' to me—why should I not say it? I am so proud of it. She is very faithful and forgiving and sweet; she would be the same, I think, if I—were even—a lackey. But I? I was a dolt, a little unsensible brute; I did not value such thing' then; I was too yo'ng, las' June. So I say to my cousin, 'No, I make my own choosing!' 'Little fool,' he answer, 'she is the one for you. Am I not wiser than you?' And he was very angry, and, as he has influence in France, word come' that he will get me put in Vincennes, so I mus' run away quick till his anger is gone. My good frien' Mirepoix is jus' leaving for London; he take' many risk' for my sake; his hairdresser die before he start', so I travel as that poor barber. But my cousin is a man to be afraid of when he is angry, even in England, and I mus' not get my Mirepoix in trouble. I mus' not be discover' till my cousin is ready to laugh about it all and make it a joke. And there may be spies; so I change my name again, and come to Bath to amuse my retreat with a little gaming—I am al—ways fond of that. But three day' ago M. le Marquis send me a courier to say that my brother, who know where I had run away, is come from France to say that my cousin is appease'; he need me for his little theatre, the play cannot go on. I do not need to espouse mademoiselle. All shall be forgiven if I return, and my brother and M. de Mirepoix will meet me in Bath to felicitate.

"There is one more thing to say, that is all. I have said I learn' a secret, and use it to make a man introduce me if I will not tell. He has absolve' me of that promise. My frien's, I had not the wish to ruin that man. I was not receive'; *Meestaire* Nash had reboff me; I had no other way excep' to use this fellow. So I say, 'Take me to Lady Malbourne's ball as "Chateaurien."' I throw off my wig, and shave, and behol', I am M. le Duc de Castle Nowhere. Ha, ha! You see?"

The young man's manner suddenly changed. He became haughty, menacing. He stretched out his arm, and pointed at Winterset. "Now I am no 'Beaucaire,' messieurs. I am a French gentleman. The man who introduce' me at the price of his honor, and then betray' me to redeem it, is that coward, that card-cheat there!"

Winterset made a horrible effort to laugh. The gentlemen who surrounded him fell away as from pestilence. "A French gentleman!" he sneered savagely, and yet fearfully. "I don't know who you are. Hide behind as many toys and ribbons as you like; I'll know the name of the man who dares bring such a charge!"

"Sir!" cried de Mirepoix sharply, advancing a step towards him; but he checked himself at once. He made a low bow of state, first to the young Frenchman, then to Lady Mary and the company. "Permit me, Lady Mary and gentlemen," he said, "to assume the honor of presenting you to His Highness, Prince Louis-Philippe de Valois, Duke of Orleans, Duke of Chartres, Duke of Nemours, Duke of Montpensier, First Prince of the Blood Royal, First Peer of France, Lieutenant-General of French Infantry, Governor of Dauphiné, Knight of the Golden Fleece, Grand Master of the Order of Notre Dame, of Mount Carmel, and of St. Lazarus in Jerusalem; and cousin to His most Christian Majesty, Louis the Fifteenth, King of France."

"Those are a few of my brother's names," whispered Henri of Beaujolais to Molyneux. "Old Mirepoix has the long breath, but it take' a strong man two day' to say all of them. I can suppose this Winterset know' now who bring the charge!"

"Castle Nowhere!" gasped Beau Nash, falling back upon the burly prop of Mr. Bantison's shoulder.

"The Duke of Orleans will receive a message from me within the hour!" said Winterset, as he made his way to the door. His face was black with rage and shame.

"I tol' you that I would not soil my hand with you," answered the young man. "If you send a message no gentleman will bring it. Whoever shall bear it will receive a little beating from François."

He stepped to Lady Mary's side. Her head was bent low, her face averted. She seemed to breathe with difficulty, and leaned heavily upon a

113

chair. "Monseigneur," she faltered in a half whisper, "can you—forgive me? It is a bitter—mistake—I have made. Forgive."

"Forgive?" he answered, and his voice was as broken as hers; but he went on, more firmly: "It is—nothing—less than nothing. There is— only jus' one—in the—whole worl' who would not have treat' me the way that you treat' me. It is to her that I am goin' to make reparation. You know something, Henri? I am not goin' back only because the king forgive' me. I am goin' to *please* him; I am goin' to espouse mademoiselle, our cousin. My frien's, I ask your felicitations."

"And the king does not compel him!" exclaimed young Henri.

"Henri, you want to fight me?" cried his brother sharply. "Don' you think the King of France is a wiser man than me?"

He offered his hand to Lady Mary.

"Mademoiselle is fatigue'. Will she honor me?"

He walked with her to the door, her hand fluttering faintly in his. From somewhere about the garments of one of them a little cloud of faded rose-leaves fell, and lay strewn on the floor behind them. He opened the door, and the lights shone on a multitude of eager faces turned toward it. There was a great hum of voices, and, over all, the fiddles wove a wandering air, a sweet French song of the *voyageur*.

He bowed very low, as, with fixed

115

and glistening eyes, Lady Mary Carlisle, the Beauty of Bath, passed
slowly by him and went out of the
room.

THE END